I0456796

MARS CALLING

GARY CARTER

This is a work of fiction. Names, characters, places, and incidents are products of the author's imagination or are used fictitiously and are not to be construed as real. Any resemblance to actual events, locations, organizations, or persons, living or dead, is entirely coincidental.

World Castle Publishing, LLC
Pensacola, Florida
Copyright © Gary Carter 2021
Paperback ISBN: 9781955086738
eBook ISBN: 9781955086745
First Edition World Castle Publishing, LLC, September 5, 2021
http://www.worldcastlepublishing.com

Licensing Notes
All rights reserved. No part of this book may be used or reproduced in any manner whatsoever without written permission, except in the case of brief quotations embodied in articles and reviews.
Cover: Karen Fuller
Editor: Maxine Bringenberg

DEDICATION

To Kimberly, Richard, and the millions of Mars fans worldwide, and to the memory of Ray Bradbury, my favorite, all time science fiction writer.

CHAPTER 1

Fresno, California

Luis Bellandia wiped his brow, hoisted his bag of Valencia oranges over his right shoulder, then worked his way down the long, wobbly extension ladder. It was July in California, and especially hot in the San Joaquin Valley, where he worked as a field hand when there were crops to be picked. He figured it to be somewhere over a hundred degrees now, with the late afternoon sun beating down on him, his coworkers, and everyone else, he reasoned, that lived in Fresno and elsewhere in the valley.

He unshouldered his oranges, laid them at the trunk of the large orange tree, and then reached for the canteen of water there, one of three he had brought with him today, the other two now empty. Grasping the canteen, he took his sombrero off and poured some of the lukewarm water over his head, then drank what was left. It was quitting time, near six in the afternoon, and time to head toward the weigh station, a good three football fields away. It had been a long day, rising from bed at five in the morning, getting dressed, eating a quick breakfast of oatmeal and milk, then kissing his wife, Jo Anne, who had risen with him and made him a sparse lunch before he left. Jo Anne worked as a kitchen helper in a local restaurant and, while her day wasn't as long as her husband's, nevertheless it wore her out working in a hot kitchen, doing dishes and other menial chores. She would leave for work an hour or so after he did, and get home a couple of hours earlier, take a nap, and then prepare dinner for the both of them.

Luis picked up his heavy bag of oranges and, slinging them over his shoulder, made his way to the weigh station. He was tall for a Mexican, twenty-three years of age, well-muscled, clean-shaven, and handsome by anyone's standards. He stopped behind the other field workers, seven in all, who were ahead of him, six men and a pretty, young, stout woman, and waited his turn.

"Forty-seven and a half pounds," Raphael, one of the weigh-in men said, weighing Luis's oranges. Once weighed, he walked through a back door and dumped the fruit in a larger crate situated outside the ramshackle shed he was working in with four other men. "A good haul for you today, Luis!" he called over his shoulder. "Twelve bags. You work very hard!"

"Yes, thank you," Luis said, getting his chit a few minutes later for today's haul, too tired to say anything else. He would collect a chit each day he worked, they were tabulated on Saturday, and he would be paid cash by the paymaster, just in time to buy groceries and other essentials. He would take Sunday off, as did most of the others, and spend some valuable time with his wife, who, after much pleading and being a good worker, had been granted permission for

Sunday off by her boss, creating ill feelings among some of the others she worked with.

Luis took out his frayed wallet, put the chit inside, put the wallet back in a back pocket of his well-worn shorts, then rinsed his head off under one of two spigots outside the shed, trying to cool off, not worried any about getting the rest of his clothes wet. He would dry off soon enough before he got home.

He turned in his chit and collected his money, along with a small bag of four free large oranges, a bonus of sorts from the farm's owner to all his workers. Anxious to get home, he hurried to his bicycle, parked in the provided bike rack along with many others, unlocked it, jumped on board, and headed for home, a good three miles away, dodging heavy traffic as he pedaled slowly in the bike lane provided, too tired to try and get home in a hurry.

* * *

Luis and Jo Anne, married out of high school at age eighteen, children of poor parents, lived in a small, yellow and white striped mobile trailer with one bedroom, a kitchen, a living room — where their small computer was housed — and a bath room, one of thirty-six trailers in a rectangular lot provided by the owner. They lived there, paying rent, along with other field workers, mostly migrants from Mexico, living in similar habitats, some by themselves, others with families with young mouths to feed. Toward the south end of the rectangular, treeless lot, roughly the size and shape of a football field, more trailers sat on both sides of a dirt road that ran between them and down the middle of the lot. There sat a large, concrete block utility building that housed separate shower rooms, sinks, and toilets for men and women who lived in trailers without bathrooms, mostly families who could not afford to pay rent for a mobile home with its own bathroom.

Jo Anne, standing five-foot-six inches, slim, strong, and beautiful, with red hair and blue eyes, met Luis at the door, a cold beer in hand. She gave him a kiss and a big hug, then handed her husband the beer, which he drank in two gulps.

"Welcome home!" she said, always cheerful and outgoing, especially around her husband, who she felt worked too long and too hard.

"Thanks," Luis said after finishing the beer. He looked at Jo

Anne's carefully tended flower and vegetable garden that surrounded their home, extending out from the trailer on all sides in the three-foot spaces provided. His wife treated her plants with tender, loving care as if they were her children. Childless, they waited for the day they could make enough money to afford children.

Luis surveyed the beauty Jo Anne had created, standing out in an otherwise messy group of homes. He smiled for the first time that day, then hugged his wife again and followed her back into the cramped trailer, where they fell into their small, two seater couch.

"How was your day?" he asked, relaxing, the beer having a quick effect.

"Busy, busy, busy, what with it being a Saturday and all. Tourists in town and kids out of school."

Luis nodded, then got up and retrieved another beer from their small refrigerator. He popped the top, took a big swallow, then handed the can to his wife, who finished it off.

"What smells so good?" he asked.

"I have baked us a chicken, with some potatoes and carrots, in celebration of Saturday night! Tomorrow is Sunday, and this will be a good start to that day, here this evening with beer and a full stomach for once!"

Luis grunted his approval, then sat back down next to his wife and put his arm around her, wondering once again how he had ever won such a beautiful, hard-working, outgoing, loving and caring woman.

* * *

The next morning dawned bright and hot. Luis and Jo Anne sat at their built-into-the-kitchen-wall half-table, just big enough to seat two people, finishing their scrambled eggs and tortillas. Luis was reading the Sunday edition of the *Fresno Bee*, the Sunday morning edition being one of the luxuries he afforded himself, not subscribing to the weekly papers. An avid reader, he would have ordered the Monday through Saturday editions had he the money and the time to read them.

He folded the paper in his lap and turned to look at his wife, who was seated to his right nursing a cup of coffee and enjoying their so far quiet, peaceful morning.

"They are advertising again," he said wistfully.

"Who?" Jo Anne asked,

recognizing her husband's look, and knew full well "*who.*"

"Sparaxis. They are asking for workers again to go to Mars. Men to work in the mines and women in the clinic, and the greenhouses, and headquarters, and the mines too, if they can do the work."

"We've talked about this before," Jo Anne said, frowning, scrutinizing her husband. "I don't know if I could survive on a dead planet, Luis. I would miss my garden, and the rain, the orange and other trees, and — well, all those things."

"The main dome, the one that protects the row houses, and the hospital, and the headquarters and other buildings, they have a park in the middle of all of them, connected by pathways. I told you this. We have seen pictures. With trees and grass and even flowers, and the greenhouses are always packed with plants. There is space between the blocks of row houses for people to plant their own gardens, grow some of their own food. We will only be gone for three years, sweetheart, three Earth years. A hundred-thousand-dollars apiece for you and me, each year, not counting the six months out and back on the ship, for which we don't get paid. That's four-hundred-thousand dollars when we are done with our tour. *Four-hundred-thousand-dollars*, Jo! We can come back and go to college, like we always dreamed, make something of ourselves, our lives, be somebody! Have children! We have no family here. There is nothing to keep us here! Please, Jo, it is our only hope."

"I don't know, Luis. I just don't know. I'm sorry. It's risky. We might not come back at all. What in the world do they mine there, that makes it profitable for old man John Sparaxis and his company?"

"Diamonds, Jo. Reds and blues, and others, rare here on Earth. And gold—very expensive now that Earth is running out—and other rare metals and things. They even bring back Mars rocks for people who want souvenirs, and for museums and such, and they sell for big prices! The old man is making another fortune by being there, all right, by being there on Mars."

"I don't know, Luis. It scares me. So many things could go wrong."

"Do you really want to be a kitchen maid all your life?" Luis asked, suddenly angry. "And me picking grapes and oranges all the time, in this terrible heat? And lettuce and crap in the winter when it is cold and foggy? What happens when we get too old to do these things? Huh? What do we do then?"

Jo Anne bowed her head, put her hands over her eyes, let out a long sigh, then raised her head and looked at her husband.

"It means that much to you? To go to that ungodly planet and work in the mines?"

"Yes, Jo Anne. It means that much to me. And it should to you, too. It is the only way we can have a future."

Jo Anne sighed again and looked at her calloused hands, the bruise on her elbow, felt the pain nagging at her lower back. Could things really get worse? Roasting in the summer and freezing in the winter? Never enough money to go anywhere or do anything, to buy the necessary clothes and food, to own their very own car?

"Well, we've got nothing to lose, I guess because we don't have much," she said, taking a deep breath. "It will be our life's great, grand adventure, something to tell our kids about."

Luis turned and grabbed his wife, hugged her tight, and kissed her forehead. "Thank you, Jo. I love you so much."

"Ouch! Don't squeeze me so hard, Luis. You'll break me!"

Luis let go and wiped at his eyes. Getting up, he jumped up and down and around, punching at the air with his fists, hooting and screaming all the while.

"Goodness sakes, Luis. Calm down! You'll have a heart attack."

"Too young for that!" he said, still dancing around the small room and boxing the air.

"Don't we have to get physicals and stuff before we can go? Pass some tests or something?"

"We are young and strong, and that is pretty much all that is required for the jobs we can do, from what I understand," Luis answered, coming over to hug his wife again. "And a willingness to sacrifice and work hard. They are having trouble finding unskilled people like us to go there."

Why am I not surprised? Jo Anne thought to herself, feeling out of sorts and uncomfortable with the idea of leaving her home, her garden, and her beautiful planet to venture to a dead planet where she was sure danger existed around every corner.

"No problem with the scientists and NASA and those kinds of people, though. They have more volunteers than they can accommodate," Luis continued. "Yahoo!" he shouted. "Mars, look out! Here we come!"

Jo Anne, filled with misgivings and foreboding, only wished she could share her husband's enthusiasm. *I will just have to learn to adapt,* she thought. *And yes, college and children might be worth the sacrifice, and fear, of leaving Earth. Only time will tell.*

CHAPTER 2

Bakersfield, California

Luis gave notice at his worksite that he would be gone for several days. Jo Anne did the same at her place of employment. Their employers weren't happy but allowed them to go, thinking they needed some time off together. Neither one told the truth of why they were going to Bakersfield, especially now, in the heat of summer.

"We are going to see a sick friend," Luis told his foreman, and Jo Anne, her boss. They rented a car at one of the Fresno lots and drove south, leaving home at five in the morning to beat the heat and arriving at the spaceport two hours later.

"Oh, my," Jo Anne said, in complete awe of the immense span of the spaceport, the enormous rockets on their platforms, the early morning sun reflecting off their sleek, metallic bodies. "I had no idea...."

"Wow," Luis said as they drove to the main entrance gate. "The pictures in the books do not even compare to what we are seeing."

"Those ships, they're beautiful, and yet scary at the same time. How do those things ever get off the ground?"

"They have all the latest designs and engines, Jo, but don't ask me how they work, and just wait until we get into space and on to the *Earthstar*, our ship to Mars. She is supposed to be five times as large as those shuttles we are looking at."

Minutes later, they arrived at the main gate, guarded by several uniformed men and women.

"Why are you here?" one of the guards, a tall, strong-looking black man, asked as he bent to look into the car from the driver's side.

"We have come to see if we are qualified to be on board the next rocket to Mars," Luis answered.

"Your names?" the guard asked, looking the duo over.

"Luis and Jo Anne Bellandia," Luis answered. Jo Anne leaned over to get a better look at the guard.

The guard punched some words into his wrist computer, looked at it, then back at Luis.

"Your social security cards?"

Luis and Jo Anne retrieved their

cards from the glove compartment and handed them to the guard, who checked the numbers and handed them back to the Bellandias.

"You're cleared to go in," the guard said and smiled. "Good luck!" he added, backing away and waving them through the opening gate.

Once inside, Luis pulled off the road and parked. Jo Anne retrieved a map of the base they had received over their computer and traced the roads that led to the immense building that housed the complex headquarters. Their appointment was at nine, and they were early, so they parked their car in a huge parking lot where they guessed close to another two hundred vehicles were parked, including trucks and cars, mobile homes, and fifth wheels. Once they had found a spot, both of them, showing signs of nervousness, walked to the main entrance of the two-story concrete and glass building, which consisted of six very wide sliding glass doors.

Inside, finding their way to the receptionist's desk, they marveled at the photos, paintings, and drawings on the walls depicting the myriad of space ships, crew members, planets, passengers, and most of all, the settlement at Bradbury Base, where they would be going were they accepted.

"You must be the Bellandias," the receptionist said, smiling and shuffling some papers on her desk. Dark of skin and hair, pretty and wearing a fluffy blue and white dress, Luis and Jo Anne recognized her as of Hispanic origin, which made the couple feel at ease. "Please, have a seat," the middle-aged woman said, pointing at the two leather chairs situated in front of her desk.

"Thank you," Jo Anne said as she and Luis took their seats.

"My name is Maria Gonzales. Welcome to the Sparaxis Spaceport!" she said, still smiling. "I have a few questions, and then I'll send you on your way. You will need to take physical and psychiatric examinations, and we will notify you within the week as to whether you have passed them or not. Now, what would you like to do on Mars? I have a copy of your email here, and it says you will consider whatever is offered that you qualify for. Is that correct?"

"Yes," Luis and Jo Anne said in unison.

"Luis, you wish to work in the mines?"

"Yes. That is about all I am

qualified for. Manual labor."

"Good. You certainly look strong enough," Maria said, smiling at Luis and unsettling Jo Anne, a streak of jealousy surging through her.

"And you, Jo Anne. You would prefer to work in the greenhouses if you have a choice? What are your credentials? Your background?"

"Uh," Jo Anne said. "I…well, I like plants. I grow a lot of them."

"She's very good with plants!" Luis interjected, seeing the worried look on his wife's face.

"Will you take another position if there are no vacancies in the greenhouses?"

"I…. Well, I suppose so if I have to," Jo Anne answered, not at all happy with the question and her answer.

"Good!" Maria said, smiling all the while. "Well, we are done here. Jo

Anne, you go down the hall to room 332 for your physical, and Luis, to the room across the hall, number 333. They are waiting for you. Once done there they will direct you to your psychiatric exam locations. One more question: if one of you is accepted and the other is not, will you still want to go?"

"That is not going to happen," Luis said, surprised at the question. "Why would any couple want to do that?"

"You will be surprised. The money, you know. Other couples have stayed apart for the three years, just for the money. Well, anyway, thank you, and good luck to you both!"

"Thank you," Luis said, helping JoAnne out of her chair. Together they walked hand in hand down the long, narrow, highly decorated hallway with more pictures of Mars and the solar system, Luis with excitement in his heart, Jo Anne with trepidation in hers.

Six days later, Luis got the email they were waiting for. He and JoAnne had passed the tests and had been accepted for the next flight to Mars, to occur in thirty days. They were required to be at Sparaxis Base in seven days, where they would undergo orientation. They would be indoctrinated with twenty-eight other people, twenty men and eight women, standard orientation class size for those making the journey. Two hundred and seventy people in all, not counting crew members, would be taking the trip together.

I am sorry, Jo Anne, Maria had said in the email, *but there are no openings in the greenhouses for you, so we have found you a place in the mess hall kitchen there, replacing one of the returnees. If this is not satisfactory, please contact us immediately so we can arrange for someone to take your place.*

"Shit! That's just great!" Jo Anne said, angry and upset at the news. "I don't want to do that! I'm not going!"

"Jo Anne, please. It will be all right," Luis consoled. "Think of the money, and our future, and maybe…. Maybe, when the next ship comes, and people go back, there will be an opening in the greenhouses. Who knows what can happen? They have put you where you are most skilled, sweetheart. It is what they do. What they have to do."

"Crap," Jo Anne said, not at all happy. "Same crummy job, just a shitty, crappy, different place."

* * *

Once orientation was finished, and everyone had passed the tests they were given, the 270 inductees, including doctors and nurses, engineers, mechanics, miners and the like, to replace their counterparts on Mars, would board the shuttle *Columbus*, take off, and dock with the *Earthstar*, now orbiting Earth. There they would be transferred to join thirty other people, twenty-five men and five women, who would be the ship's crew members assigned to various jobs aboard the *Earthstar*. Once aboard and indoctrinated, the passengers would be shown their berths, women in one room with bunk beds and a single, large, multi-stalled bathroom with toilets and sinks, the men in another, larger room with two large bath rooms. Any married couples would share small, 10'x10' rooms with bunk beds, a dresser, and a small closet. They would have to use the communal bathrooms down the hall with the others.

Once settled in and the *Columbus* headed back home, the *Earthstar* would fire up her nuclear-powered engines and set course for Mars, the trip out to take around six months. Once in Mars orbit, they would dock with the shuttle *Odyssey*, board her in units, load supplies for Bradbury Base, and travel down to the Martian surface, landing a mile away from the settlement at the spaceport there. Once docked, the passengers would be the first to depart for Bradbury Base to get settled in. Next, supplies aboard the *Odyssey* would be transported to various places at the spaceport for use at the settlement and to where they were needed at the NASA and United Nations Terraforming Outposts (UNTO) bases that were stationed around the planet. Once that was done, the shuttle would take those people whose contracts were up and ferry them back to the *Earthstar*, along with several tons of precious, expensive minerals from the mines and elsewhere, along with Mars rocks that people would pay hundreds, even thousands, of dollars to keep as souvenirs.

There would be two trips down from the *Odyssey*, each carrying around 135 passengers and restocking supplies each time, and two trips back, carrying around 135 passengers back to the *Earthstar* along with gold, diamonds and other precious minerals and rocks, where they would be stored in the empty cargo spaces that the supplies down to Mars had occupied.

The 270 or so passengers going back on the *Earthstar*, most of whom were happy that their two earth-year stints on the planet were finished, included the three men that had been killed in the mines.

CHAPTER 3

On Board the *Earthstar*

The trip up to the *Earthstar* on the *Columbus* proved exhilarating for some and frightening for others, but once the shuttle had docked safely alongside the *Earthstar* and its passengers had been escorted through the tunnel connecting the two ships with help from crew members, things settled down some. The new arrivals had made their way to the orientation room, using hand holds along the circular walls. There they strapped themselves into chairs to keep from floating away, trying to get used to zero gravity as they listened to crew members explaining what was ahead of them and what was expected of them. They were all issued interior maps of the *Earthstar*, explaining what was where and how to get there and what their shifts for meals, sleeping, exercising, and working, among other things, would be.

Once that was done, the *Earthstar* fired up her engines and established her trajectory toward Mars, pushing people back into their cushioned seats for close to two hours. The newly arrived passengers, growing weary from being squashed in their seats, unstrapped themselves and exited the room as best they could, floating off in different directions, spinning and turning until they could find a hand hold and stabilize themselves, much to the amusement of the seasoned crew members. Once oriented, the new arrivals, ship maps in hand, made their way to their assigned quarters, some of them becoming dizzy and nauseous with the loss of gravity and the spinning around, but soon rescued and helped along by crew members until they reached their assigned living quarters.

* * *

Once situated in their room, the Bellandias looked around at their cramped quarters. Bolted along one eight-foot wall were their bunk beds, complete with blankets and straps to hold them in when sleeping. On the opposite side was a wooden dresser containing two drawers, one containing small, plastic, sealed pouches with straws and water in them, along with a box of strapped-down napkins. There were two radiation suits in the other, larger drawer. On top of the dresser, bolted down, was a small TV screen, with an attached two-way intercom for viewing assorted TV channels from Earth and calling for help, or talking to crew members, if needed.

Once situated, the Bellandias quickly shed their outer clothes, pulled out the radiation suits, stuffed their Earth clothes in the same drawer, closed it, and then donned the uncomfortable radiation suits provided, one having the words "Jo Anne Bellandia" sewn over an outer pocket, and the other the name "Luis Bellandia" with his name sewn in the same place on his suit.

"Looks like they knew we were coming," Jo Anne said, admiring her suit as best she could in the gravity-less room. "Impressive!" she added, hanging upside down in their room, using the handholds provided to keep from bouncing off the walls, into her husband, or anything else in the room.

"Pretty cramped in here," Luis said, looking around. "But better than being in a room with a lot of other men, I am sure."

"Wow, these are tight!" Jo Anne said after a while, sitting on the bottom bunk, holding on with one hand and struggling with the other, trying to get her legs into the suit. "I'm not sure I can wear these things for six months. They're already proving to be a pain in the ass. When, if ever, do we get to take the damn things off?"

"According to what I have read, we will be using wet towels to clean our bodies and waterless shampoo for our hair, and wipe off with dry towels, down the hall there. You get to take off your suit and underclothes then, and there's also a place to clean both. We will be assigned times to do this, so the bathroom is not overcrowded. You should know this."

"Sorry! I can't remember everything. I'm already not liking this trip, Luis. How do I scratch if I get an itch?"

Luis laughed. "You will take your suit off and address the itching as quick as you can, or put medicine on it, or both, and then cover back up. Too much radiation affecting us can kill us. It's that simple."

Jo Anne grunted and finally got her suit on, complete with the cap that only left her face and hands exposed to the elements inside the ship. Once that was done, she unpacked the one small cardboard box with personal items she had been allowed to bring on board. First off, she removed the small, 4″ potted, well-packed red geranium her mother had given her shortly before her mother and father had died in a car accident when Jo Anne was seventeen. After that, Jo Anne had been forced to live with her mother's sister, who didn't like her very much but was the only one who would take her in. Next, she unpacked some cosmetics along with two novels she had always wanted to read, a box of mixed candy bars, and a framed picture of her deceased parents holding her in their arms when she was only two. Had Luis not been by her side during her grief, she knew she never would have made it. She would do anything for him — including this trip to a place she did not want to go to. *A dead planet, for all intents and purposes, except for the park at Bradbury Base and the greenhouses. Nothing but a huge pile of sand and rocks.* Two years! How was she ever going to make it for that long in such a desolate place? *I hope they have plenty of beer and wine there,* she thought to herself.

After a lengthy time, Jo Anne and Luis finally, with help from each other, had their suits on and zipped up. Small flaps at the shoulders were opened to let out excessive heat, of which there probably wouldn't be too much since they kept the ship at a constant sixty-five degrees to save on energy. More flaps could be opened around their bottoms when they needed to relieve themselves.

"This sucks," Jo Anne said, scooting around the cubicle, trying to get used to her suit and comfortable in the tight fit.

"Jo Anne," Luis said, looking at his wife, wondering now if he had done the right thing in pushing her into going to Mars. "You are so negative lately. What has happened to my beautiful, positive and cheerful wife?"

Jo Anne stopped by the dresser, inserting her feet in one set of the straps set around the room, bolted to the floor, to keep its occupants "grounded," and looked at her husband of five years — her savior, her lover, her confident, her best friend. He was right. She was being way too negative. It was time to stop and move into their futures together. She unhitched her feet, floated the few steps between them, threw her arms around his neck, and held on tight.

"You're right, Luis. I've been

being a real bitch," she said, looking into his eyes after a long kiss. "No more! I promise you I will be on my best behavior for the next three years, and look forward to going back to school, and great careers, and most of all, children of our own. I promise I won't let you down. I love you way too much to hurt you anymore."

The couple kissed again, and then Jo Anne stepped back and picked her red geranium, six inches tall and three inches wide, counting the root ball, out of the box where she had tied it down beneath her other things, having removed the pot on Earth. Then she'd wrapped her plant in plastic for the journey to the *Earthstar*, none the worse for wear for the arduous journey it had been on.

"I'm going to take Louise to the greenhouse bays," Jo Anne said, perking up. "If you remember, they promised me a spot when we got here and that I could go visit her whenever I wanted to."

"Louise?"

"Yes. Louise Anne Carmichael. I have named her after my mother," Jo Anne said, smiling while picking a half-dead leaf off the plant and watching it float around the room. "You should know that!" she scolded.

Luis let out a deep breath, relieved to see his wife smile for the first time in — well, weeks since they had been accepted for the journey.

"Sorry," Luis said. "How does that work? The plant, I mean. How do you keep it alive?"

Jo Anne held up her geranium. "It will be replanted and reinforced in a type of clear plastic bag, which is called a 'pillow' and looks like one. You will be able to see the roots as it will be planted in a hydroponic medium. There will be a little straw stuck in the bag, sticking out three inches and permeating inside the pillow the same distance. The straw will have a lid that opens and closes at the top. You use an injector, like a syringe, to water Louise and add liquid nutrients on a regular schedule. You open the lid, poke the syringe into the opening, squirt the water in, pull the syringe out, and close the lid. That way, you hopefully don't lose any water or dirt into the air. That's the idea, anyway. That's how they grow food in the greenhouse to help feed us all. Got to have our greens! And tomatoes!"

"Interesting," Luis said.

"Yes. Anyway, I am going to take Louise to the greenhouse assigned to her. Would you like to come?"

"You bet," Luis answered, glad to see his wife in a better mood. *Thank God she loves plants*, he thought.

He followed her down the long, narrow, mostly circular hallway toward the front of the ship, both of them pulling or pushing themselves forward, having some difficulties along the way getting used to their new weightless environment. At one point, Jo Anne lost her geranium, grabbing at it with both hands as it floated away. Luis to the rescue. Pushing off from a hand hold, he grabbed the bag and held on tight. Jo Anne, laughing, positioned herself against the wall and took Louise from Luis, planting it under her left arm and squeezing the bag a little harder than before.

"It's a good thing this bag is airtight," she said as they maneuvered their way toward the front of the ship, dodging all manner of pipes, hoses, and other objects along the way while opening, and closing, airlock doors before and behind them every fifty yards or so.

Eventually, they came to an airlock that opened to the ship's quarter-mile long greenhouse, situated close to the nose of the ship. Vertical, clear, reflective glass walls stretched fifty yards long and eight feet high along the back walls of the room. Fifty yards long, four-foot-high and three-foot-deep wooden tables sat on either side of a well-worn centered floor. All of the connecting tables, each with two-foot deep sunken beds within their walls, were set on either side of the four-foot-wide floor and lay inside the tables. Hundreds of airbag pillows lay anchored in the beds to keep from floating off. All were filled with perlite for future plant roots, once seeds were planted, to be fed with a nutrient-rich water solution.

On reaching a closed, eight-foot-wide sliding glass door, Luis slid the door open, and he and Jo Anne floated into the room, again using the hand holds provided. There they were met by a slim, middle-aged woman, who Jo Anne guessed to be around thirty-five years of age and around five-foot-five, with light brown hair and matching eyes, and dressed in a green radiation suit.

"Hello," she said cheerfully. "You are the first ones here. Welcome! I am Doctor Melissa Yvonne Pitchford if you will, but please call me Missy. I have doctorate degrees in botany and horticulture. This will be my second trip out to Mars and back, so I have some experience and, if all goes well, I will be traveling back to Earth with you in three years or so."

Impressed, Luis and Jo Anne nodded their hellos, gave their names, and then scrutinized the long rows of benches with overhead grow lights shining down, brightening the inside hull of the ship and illuminating the pillows.

"Where are the plants?" Jo Anne asked, mystified, holding Louise close to her with one arm and holding onto a rail with the other. "I don't see any plants."

"We are growing them from seeds, watered just hours ago in their pillows, as you can see. It would be too much extra weight transporting them up from Earth already growing, and it would be hard on the plants. If all goes well, we should have fresh vegetables and fruits in a month or so, and all our passengers will be allowed to come in and look and ask questions, even help out if they so choose. A kind of oasis, if you will. Working with plants helps space people keep their sanity and mental health, as you may have heard."

"Yes!" Jo Anne said enthusiastically, brightening, awed by her surroundings. "While aboard, I have been assigned to help out in your greenhouses here on the ship, but you probably already know that. I love plants, and I'm sure it will help me from becoming bored over the next six months, and I'll learn a lot. When do I start?"

"Well, you just got here, so probably in two or three days, as you have to become used to the ship and have your indoctrinations for the do's and don'ts of our long trip. Let's see, today is Monday, so how about Thursday, 0900 hours?"

"Sounds good, but I have a question: Why do you guys use Earth days and months out here?"

"It's one way of staying locked in with our homes. It helps us to keep our minds clear and to know what seasons are going on back on Earth, when birthdays are, etc. You will find out more of the ways we keep ourselves balanced as we progress toward Mars, including your work, the daily two to three hour shifts exercising in the gym, and other things. It will not be an easy trip for any of us, even us veterans. Anyway, I will look forward to working with you, Jo Anne. Lots to learn, lots to do! We are responsible for helping to feed around three hundred people a day on our trip. If we fail, all else fails. And you, Luis, what are your plans?"

"I've been asked to help with ships' clean up. Bathrooms and such. Maintenance. I was a field hand back on Earth. No fields here!"

"No, and not on Mars either, I'm afraid. Not yet. But the outposts on Mars — including the Sparaxis mining complex, and the folks who work at the two NASA bases and the seven scattered UNTO bases, along with others from Bradbury Base, who have been working on terraforming Mars for a very long time — are hoping that one day we will have fields of corn, wheat, and everything growing all over! They are making progress, but it looks like it's going to take a long time to terraform Mars, much longer than we had hoped for."

"What's UNTO?" Luis asked.

"It stands for 'United Nations Terraforming Outpost,' one close to each polar cap, and five others spread equidistantly around the equator. Each of the bases, except the two polar ice cap outposts, also have greenhouse gas producing factories close by, which they monitor and maintain. It's a complex process and requires a lot of skill to keep them operating. So far, so good."

"Yeah, I remember now," Luis said. "They briefly mentioned them at one of our orientation classes on Earth. Said we would learn more once on our way."

"Where does Louise go?" interjected Jo Anne after securing her feet in some straps on the floor and showcasing her plant to the doctor. "She's named after my mother."

"Follow me," Melissa said,

gingerly removing the plant from Jo Anne's hands and, wearing metallic magnetic boots, walked down the narrow, magnetic strip laid along the middle of the floor separating the two sets of tables lining the large room, leaving Jo Anne and Luis to use the handholds. "You will be given magnetic boots to wear once you start work in our greenhouses," Doctor Pitchford said along the way. "Luis, you too, for your work. Even so, you both better get used to floating around."

Once at the end of the long right side tables, close to the sliding glass door there, Melissa pointed to a small area inside the sunken bench, to a pillow tagged "Bellandia."

"Here is your place," she said, pointing to a pillow. "We knew you were coming!" she added, laughing.

"You can come and go whenever you want as we are always open, and we will be very busy when our plants start to grow, as you will find out. Not that easy growing plants under artificial conditions, but they help feed us, and take in carbon dioxide and release oxygen to help us breathe. Anyway, don't worry. If you run into trouble with Louise, we will help. We will get her to Mars, safe and sound, along with you guys. I can feel how precious she is to you. I promise."

"Thank you," Jo Anne said, humbled. She slipped her feet into another set of floor straps and took Louise back from the doctor's hands, not wanting anyone else to touch or hold her, afraid of irreparable damage. "How do I do this?" she asked.

Melissa reached over and, grabbing onto a metal hand-hold

anchored to the bench, helped Jo Anne set her plant in its designated pillow and anchor it down without ripping the fabric.

"There, done!" Melissa said, smiling. "Our first plant on this long trip. Yay! Congratulations, and thanks to you both!" she said, hugging each of them and surprising both of them with her strength. "We shall become good friends on this long, arduous, and amazing trip. It will be necessary for our survival that we get along, all of us, otherwise our *Earthstar* will founder. We can fix mechanical things if they malfunction or get broken, but while we have a space psychiatrist aboard, we can't fix broken humans. Do you understand?"

"Y…yes," Jo Anne, taken aback by the warning, answered. "We…we understand." Frowning, she looked at

Luis, who nodded his head, equally disturbed by the thought.

* * *

After unwrapping, planting, securing, and blowing a kiss to a forlorn-looking Louise, Jo Anne and Luis followed Melissa on a quick tour of the greenhouse facilities. After that, they took the hallway back to their quarters, talked awhile, then went to the mess hall to be joined by some of the other three-hundred passengers and crew members on the ship, all of them having to eat in designated shifts as the dining area had room for only a hundred people at a time.

Luis and Jo Anne experienced difficulty at first, along with the others in the room, having trouble sitting with only straps to hold them on their seats and trying to consume their selected food from plastic squeeze bottles.

However, the tubed selections—placed inside small, square openings in a well-constructed, checkered wall, each compartment with a pivotal glass door—tasted good, and before long, they had mastered the art, their previous training on Earth helping out.

* * *

Later that night, Jo Anne and Luis, tired from the long day and the stress associated with it and still in their radiation outfits, strapped themselves into their bunks. Luis selected the top bunk and Jo Anne the one beneath it, pulling the single cover supplied over their bodies and then strapping in. There was no need for another cover, as the ship was kept at a constant sixty-five degrees throughout and, having to stay in their radiation suits, they were kept warm enough.

Once secured, Luis leaned over the edge of his bunk and peered down at an uncomfortable Jo Anne.

"Want to make love?" he asked, smiling. "Should be fun in no gravity."

"Luis, get serious!" Jo Anne answered. Turning away from her husband's eyes, she started giggling.

The Bellandias slept that first night fitfully, tossing and turning as best they could beneath the straps, away from home, worried yet excited about the adventure that lay before them. The vibrations from the nuclear engines, located a good half-mile aft from the main body of the ship and still firing from time to time, were not helping.

* * *

As the programmed days and nights passed, Luis and Jo Anne learned their jobs, Jo Anne ecstatic at watching Louise grow, along with the now harvestable vegetables and genetically engineered dwarf fruit trees, more fruit than plant.

Luis was not so happy with his maintenance job, especially having to clean the men's shower room and toilet setups on a daily basis.

Monotony and boredom for those on board were countered by visits to the greenhouses, chess and checkers and other board games, with magnetic pieces and magnetic boards secured to tables, which were, in turn, bolted to the floor in the large gaming room. Thin, magnetic cards were available for card games on magnetized tables. Movies were shown twice a day in the large meeting room for those off duty, a new one every day, and big-screen television programs aired in another, smaller room, delayed from Earth, for those who wanted to watch them.

There were enough people on board, playing various instruments that they had been allowed to bring along, to form a band of sorts, which they did after getting to know one another. Once a week, their feet secured to the floor or their legs to seats, depending on what instruments they played, including a bolted down piano and bench making the trip, the makeshift band played on a Saturday night, and once a week on a Wednesday night, so that all the *Earthstar*'s personnel who wanted to could come, watch, and listen when not working.

After many "concerts," as the musicians liked to call them, people who came to watch began learning to dance together, or alone, in the large room, floating around, having learned how to manage themselves in zero gravity without injuring themselves. It was a sight to see when they danced, doing somersaults, spinning around and such, and especially when they all square danced together, floating up and down and around, banging into each other, laughing and having a good time in the well-padded room.

Behind the flight officer's bridge, at the nose of the *Earthstar*, was the exercise room where all the ship's inhabitants were required to exercise each day, again in shifts, on various contraptions designed for free-fall, to keep muscle, bones, brains, and all other human tissue from deteriorating.

At the front of the ship, sitting over the bridge and the *Earthstar*'s crew quarters, sat a large, see-through, plastisteel dome, where anyone could go, at any time when not working, and gaze at the stars. They called it, appropriately enough, the "Star-Light Room." Earth and Mars were also visible. Jo Anne would go up almost every day and float around with others. She watched, her heart yearning, as her beautiful, blue and white home world shrank ever smaller, and red Mars grew ever larger. After a while, becoming depressed at what she was seeing, longing to be back home, she quit going up to the dome at all, spending spare time in the greenhouses and tending to Louise, now grown tall and wide. In the zero gravity, Louise produced large, red flowers that Jo Anne snipped and took back to her room, wrapping their stems in a wet towel and tying them to her bunk, sometimes sharing them with the other women on board, much to their delight.

CHAPTER 4

Two Months Later

UNTO Base One, Martian Northern Polar Icecap

From their planetary base, carved into a Martian hillside to ward off radiation and keep temperatures more stable, Armand Moreau, native Frenchman, watched his computer in disgust as the meteoroids tore through the space mirror that had taken mankind so many years to construct, fly to Mars and place into orbit.

"Now what do we do?" Miriam Jacobs asked. From America, she was surrounded by the other six members who lived and worked at the station. All of them were looking over Moreau's shoulders and staring, in disbelief, at the screen along with him. "It will take forever to fix. So much for piping water to Bradbury Base, not to mention the loss of our ability to keep on melting polar ice to help speed along our trying to terraform this desert planet. This is going to set everything back, and who knows for how long?"

"There is still water being piped from the southern pole," Moreau said.

"That water is allocated to the Sparaxis mining operations," Jacobs reminded him. "Old man Sparaxis funded that whole operation, otherwise there would be no mining, and Bradbury Base would not exist, leaving only UNTO and NASA to fund Mars operations and to terraform the planet."

"They have aquifers," Ivan Oblonsky, from Russia, said, "to supply the base with."

"Yes, but those will not keep that city going as it is now," Moreau said, looking over his shoulder at Oblonsky. "They will need more water than that for the greenhouses, or those living there are going to get very, very hungry, and thirsty too, with having to ration the water. Sorry to say, the rest of us will not be able to help much until we get in touch with Earth and supplies are sent to fix the mirror, which will take months, maybe even a year or more, and delay the repair of the mirror to help keep Bradbury Base, and its greenhouses, heated, not to mention the water issue."

"And us? What about us?" Henrietta Romero, from Mexico, asked. "We use water from the pole, too."

"We have backup tanks," Moreau answered, "and our own aquifer and our two rovers can take us to the polar ice fields to dig ice and bring it back here to melt and use, and may be able to process enough ice to help the base, too. It won't be easy for anyone, but we are better adapted to survive than the first humans to arrive here and colonize Mars. We should be okay until our materials arrive. We have some material, but not enough to replace the whole mirror. We will just have to wait and do the best we can."

"Poor Bradbury Base," Jacobs said, frowning. "I'm afraid they are going to have a rough time of it for a while."

"A very long while," Moreau added, "along with the rest of us."

CHAPTER 5

Bradbury Base, Mars

Ten Months Later

Tired, worried, and increasingly disenchanted, Luis stepped from the solar-powered minibus, his miner's helmet tucked under his right arm, and winced as currents of cold, stale, recycled air pushed against his face and the heavily insulated miner's outfit he was wearing.

"Damn engineers," he mumbled, pulling his suit up against

the chill. Stopping momentarily, Luis looked up at the massive dome protecting Bradbury Base and shook his fist toward its apex, cursing all the while. Then, feeling better, he turned and faced the bus. "Adios!" he yelled, leaning in the bus doorway. Luis waved goodbye to the driver and a few of his coworkers still inside. "I hope you all manage not to freeze tonight, my friends. Then I will not only inherit your jobs but your women as well! Those of you that are lucky enough to have one, eh?"

His coworkers laughed, and soon the yellow, blue, and purple painted vehicle was back on its route around the dome, kicking up pink gravel and dust on the way. Luis followed its path for a few moments until the minibus disappeared behind a row of dead cottonwood trees.

Broken branches and limbs lay about their base, scattered among dead shrubs and flowers, vivid reminders of better days. Frowning, he turned and limped onto the sidewalk leading to his two-story rectangular row-house, nestled between other row-houses on the same block.

High overhead, toward the apex of the two-chambered, silica-aerogel filled circular dome walls, and outside, a trio of scrubbers were working, two men and a woman, outfitted in fluorescent green radiation-proof pressure suits. They dangled precariously from safety harnesses attached to the main solar array, one of three three-hundred-foot tall steel posts that supported the colony's huge communication disks. With backpack blowers strapped on, they swung back and forth, trying to clear the dome of dust and grit, a never-ending job. Eight months or so ago, when the afternoons were warm enough, the dome had been pressure-washed, back when water was deemed plentiful, and its evaporation into the thin atmosphere was considered useful in helping to terraform the arid world. But since then, the city's complex system of plumbing and sprinkler systems had been shut down because of the water shortage. Now, with the precious liquid strictly rationed because of the still torn space mirror, taking longer to fix than originally estimated, the occupants of Bradbury Base were worried about their future and whether or not their domed city, and those that lived within it, would survive long enough for the mirror to become functional, and revive the base before things inside the dome got worse.

The blowing was proving ineffective, Luis noted, for it seemed the city was still forever blanketed beneath a haze of fine, red dust, obscuring much of the already weak light that reached the city from far off Sol, which helped to warm the dome during the daylight hours. But the job had to be done. Leave the dust and grit to accumulate, and the dome would lose its greenhouse effect, further paralyzing the mining colony.

Luis continued along the pebbled walkway, the tiny stones a pinkish-red, in concert with most everything else on Mars. The evening was already cold, distant Sol beginning its downward spiral behind the sixteen-mile high volcano, Olympus Mons, which sat several miles to the west of the base. As if things weren't bad enough with the space mirror still not functioning, two of the company's kilo power nuclear reactors had gone down recently, keeping the base engineers and mechanics busier than they wanted to be, afraid of a complete shutdown. Now Bradbury Base was rationing energy too, the solar panels surrounding most of the base, and the geothermal well inside the dome, unable to pick up the slack. People slept fitfully, worried that the remaining reactors might fail and wondering how they would survive should that event occur.

"*Dios mio*," Luis muttered, shivering as he reached the door of his narrow, two-story, red-brick row house. "It is summer now, but who can tell?"

He paused at the doorway and glanced around at the withered

lawns, the dead trees and shrubs, exported as seeds and seedlings from Earth at great expense to the corporation, back when the dome was finally completed, and things were just getting started. His heart sagged along with the decaying flowers and trees, the grasses and ground covers. *Dead and red*, he thought. *Everything on Mars is dead and red.* Not so long ago, several years after the town had been fully settled and the mines were running at full power, before the space mirror had been shredded and the waterline to the base frozen, no longer useful, Bradbury Base had flourished with majestic, genetically enhanced trees, flowers, herbs, victory gardens, and lush, beautiful, green hybrid Bermuda grass lawns. The air had been warm and humid then, the dome and greenhouses kept warm during daylight hours by distant Sol, and warmed during night time by the nuclear reactors and the geothermal well. Verdant trees had ringed Main Street and dominated Central Park, living trees of every size and shape and color rustling against the indoor thermals, whispering of Earth and taking some of the sting out of being so damn far away from home. But the pipeline had quit carrying water around eight months ago, making things miserable for the inhabitants of Bradbury Base.

The colony had almost gone to war with UNTO over that one. Part of their job was to look after the space mirrors and keep them functioning. Then the aquifer that backed up the city and the greenhouses had become overtaxed, its levels drawn dangerously low. With no moisture from the north to replenish the underground water, NASA's mining authority had been forced to ration the precious liquid, most of it going to greenhouse crops to keep them alive and keep Bradbury Base, UNTO, and NASA citizens from going hungry and possibly starving. Now watering anything inside the dome was taboo, had been for a long time, and what water the inhabitants used was recycled over and over and over, having taken on a foul-smelling odor, making them feel uneasy every time they used it for drinking and washing.

That—along with the liquid gold thawed from the underground ice at enormous cost, plus what water from the South Pole the mines could spare, along with ice trucked in from the North Pole—was all that kept the city going. Use of in-home toilets, sinks, and bathtubs had been outlawed months ago, and the local citizenry made do with ration cards for drinking water, trips to outhouses, and the corporation laundromat and bathhouse for their personal needs. People didn't live in Bradbury Base anymore — they existed and were waiting anxiously for the mirror and the reactors to get fixed.

Luis sighed and turned his attention to the door. The six-day, sixty-hour week at the mines had worn him out. He wasn't as strong anymore, not since the accident when he had tripped and hurt his left knee, still in a knee brace. Thankfully tomorrow was his day off, and he could rest. He had hidden a small bottle of champagne under his housecoat in the entrance closet. The bottle had cost him a small fortune in credits, but he felt the monetary effort worthwhile and necessary. Tonight would be special, for it marked his and Jo Anne's fifth wedding anniversary. Almost as important, it left only another twenty months on their two-year contract on the planet, and since they counted each month as it passed, it was a milestone of sorts. Then, when their time was up, they would return to Earth with enough money to go to college, have children, and start a new life. This was their dream. This was their hope. This was what they worried about, sweated and sacrificed for.

Luis wiped his feet on the disintegrating doormat, leaving a fine coat of powdered dust beneath his boots. He opened the purple plastic door and entered, feeling relief as lukewarm air washed over him. He closed the door quietly, then hung his helmet, crawled out of his overcoat and the mining suit beneath it, then hung them in the closet inside the doorway. After donning a pair of warm sweats, a sweater, an overcoat, and a woolen cap, he tiptoed toward the small living room, the bottle of champagne held behind him, hoping to surprise his wife.

Jo Anne, who usually arrived home before he did, worked as a kitchen helper at the corporation complex within the park. Since both their days were long and unpredictable, she often took naps before their evening meal. His wife hadn't taken naps when they had first arrived, Luis remembered, or afterward for that matter, embracing Mars and their future together with all the gusto and enthusiasm that a beautiful, robust, and excitable young woman could muster. But since the water supply had proved inadequate for everything, the trees and other plants dying over time, it seemed Jo Anne's spirit had died along with them. Now, much to his dismay, when not working at the complex, she spent most of her spare time sleeping or staring out the living room window. She had become withdrawn and reclusive as the seldom-changing Martian days and nights plodded by. Luis was scared. He could only guess at why his once cheerful and outgoing wife had withdrawn inside herself. The precious champagne would bolster her spirits. He was sure of it. Maybe they would even make love again once a few drinks were down. It had been a long time. Too long.

Luis proceeded through the narrow entryway and into the living room. His row house, like every one of the three-hundred other row houses that circled inside the dome, all of which were constructed, for the most part, from bricks made from Martian soil, consisted of five small rooms. Down-ladder was the small entryway and its attendant closet. This, in turn, connected to a kitchen-dining area and the living room, sparsely furnished by the corporation. Up-ladder was the bedroom, a closet, and the now nonfunctional bathroom. There was no stairwell, simply a ladder up and down. Both up-ladder and down-ladder rooms were six-hundred feet square, same as every other row house on Bradbury Base. Each home had a small living room window that faced the lower section of the transparent, curving dome some hundred feet away.

The Bellandia home, facing

west, had a ringside view of massive Olympus Mons, the largest volcano in the solar system. Cramped and crowded, nevertheless, their row house contained more square feet of living space than either Luis or Jo Anne had ever lived in back on overcrowded Earth.

Luis gazed out the window for a minute, taking in the red, sandy, and rock-strewn plain beyond with only impressive sixteen-mile-high Olympus Mons to break the monotony. Startled, he noticed the newly formed wispy clouds around its base and what looked like new-fallen snow above that, creating a beautiful panorama against the pink sky. In awe, he attributed the scene to the ongoing arduous task of trying to terraform the planet and said a small, silent prayer that maybe things were going to work out after all. *If only they can get the pipeline working again before things completely fall apart,* he thought.

Centered in the middle of the once flourishing park lay the corporation's headquarters that included a cafeteria, laundromat, infirmary, company store, shower stalls, outhouses, a commissary, and a small bar, once the planetary hot spot. Now the differing factions, NASA and UNTO, stressed by the lack of water that they were forced to share with Bradbury Base, all of it having to be delivered on Rovers jimmied with trash cans, barrels, metal boxes and other containers that would hold water, were worried about surviving more than anything, causing them to be sorely set against one another. They rarely intermingled anymore, a sad fact considering where they were and how few people populated the planet.

Bradbury Base had been constructed on a plateau that gave its residents a 360-degree view of their surroundings and allowed more sunlight to reach the greenhouses as, except for towering Olympus Mons to the west, there were no higher hills or other volcanoes in the immediate vicinity to shade them. Three airlocks marred the otherwise smooth surface of the dome at its base, the smallest on the east side that opened on a mile long road that wound down the plateau and ended at the entrance to a series of natural underground caverns where, thirty-seven years ago, the Sparaxis Corporation had first set up shop, and which now housed the planet's storehouse for incoming supplies and its precious minerals being sent back to Earth, and was a staging area for the people going home, whose contracted time with the corporation was over. A huge, level, graded area, close to the caves, harbored Bradbury Bases' spaceport, where the shuttle *Odyssey* landed to offload passengers and supplies and subsequently transported diamonds, gold, and other precious minerals and rocks back up to the *Propitious*, sister ship to the *Earthstar*, along with those people whose two-year contracts were up.

The *Odyssey* sat there now, on the outskirts of the spaceport, having arrived just yesterday. After offloading some of the new arrivals first thing, the base's huge transport Rover sat beside the ship, its crew and captain busy loading her with the much needed supplies to be delivered to the dome and over to the mines, with backup supplies going into the caves for future use. Once that was done, NASA and UNTO would come and pick up the supplies they needed, drop off any of their returnees, pick up their replacements in surface transport vehicles, and take them back to their bases, including UNTO's critical materials to finish repairing the space mirror and get Bradbury Base's desperately needed water flowing again.

A northern airlock connected to a large domed tunnel, a quarter-mile long, that connected to a half-dozen expansive greenhouses where the food was grown that helped feed UNTO, NASA, and Bradbury Base, and which were now consuming most of the base's available water and what energy they needed, to keep the plants alive and the people they fed from starving.

The third, more massive airlock lay on the northwest perimeter, a large, enclosed sky-lift terminal. There, two pressurized and radiation-proof boxcars rode the high cables, transporting mine workers and supplies back and forth, down over the crags and overhangs of the plateau's western perimeter and across the sandy, usually windswept plain to terminate at the only entrance to the mines, a distance of several miles. The mine's entryway, another massive airlock, was lost against the staggering six-mile high lava escarpment that comprised the eastern flank of Olympus Mons. The view of the mountain from Bradbury Base was both impressive and beautiful to its residents, the mass of the sixteen-mile-high volcano, almost four times the height of Mount Everest back on Earth, dominating the western skyline.

Surrounding headquarters was Sparaxis Park, named for the corporation's founder, Max Foster Sparaxis, patriarch of the Earth trillionaire Sparaxis family. Max owned and operated just about everything ownable on Mars, short of UNTO and their terraforming projects and the two planetary bases operated by NASA.

Once lush and green, the park's small lake and artificial stream had long ago turned to cobbles and dust, its trees and grasses and shrubs withered and dried and dead. Despite the well-kept walkways, public amphitheater, basketball court with its fifteen-foot backboards, and other public amenities, the area had lost its attraction, and few Bradbury Base residents went there anymore, especially on those too frequent nights when the remaining nuclear power plants all but failed against the cold. The park had reverted to its desert heritage, same as the victory gardens, the flower beds, the lawns, and everything else, depressing everyone.

"Jo?" Luis said as he tiptoed through the entryway. "'Jo, I have a surprise!"

Luis walked into the main room and found his wife sitting there on an old black, badly scratched, flimsy plastic chair, staring out across the barren Martian landscape through the one window allowed in their down-ladder room. Off in the hazy distance, Luis could see distant Sol fading farther behind Olympus Mons, shades of pink and orange sprinkled against the sky behind the mountain. Bright lights twinkled at the volcano's base, lighting up the industrial complex and illuminating long spumes of white smoke rising against the impossibly high cliff faces.

"Jo?" he asked again, his handsome, Hispanic face clothed half in smile, half in fear. He moved beside her, noticing the small, strong hands folded neatly in her lap, a ghostly white, holding onto each other with a deathlike grip. He waved the bottle of champagne in front of Jo Anne's eyes.

"Jo Anne!" he shouted finally, perplexed, angry, and hurt when she failed to notice him. No man liked being ignored, especially by his own wife, and it seemed as if lately, this was becoming more and more the case.

"Wake up, Jo! I am home!" he shouted again, then, upset with himself, spoke in a gentler, quieter voice. "Sweetheart, I am sorry. Are you all right? Is something the matter?" Luis put his free hand to her chin, lifted it, and gazed into vacant, non-seeing eyes. "Talk to me!"

Jo Anne blinked. Her eyes lost their waxy gleam. She stared at her husband for a moment before recognition set in.

"Luis?"

"Who else could it be?" Luis answered with a puzzled frown. Dark, troubled eyes peered out from his strong brown face, questioning. Still holding her chin, he bent over and kissed her softly on the lips. "Tell me you are all right," he said, then let go and backed away.

Jo Anne's hands released their

death grip on one another and went to her unkempt long, wavy red hair and fussed there, trying to tidy the errant strands for her man. Her eyes darted into his and then back out the window again, surveying the endless expanse of lifeless desert. Off in the distance, well beyond the mountain and its necklace of lights, the vast landscapes of sand, craters, rocks, and volcanic ejecta died beneath a blotchy sun. Jo Anne searched for birds along the horizon, for kites, an airplane, a contrail, anything, and came up empty, as empty as her heart had become when the trees, flowers, and other plants, along with her victory garden, had withered and died. She felt as if the same thing had happened to her, and as hard as she tried, Jo Anne couldn't shake her mounting depression.

Jo Anne stood abruptly and pulled at her fading yellow coat with the missing buttons, then turned and walked the few short steps to a pink, plastic half-table set against a wall that badly needed painting. She began fussing with a small bouquet of dried flowers there, flowers that had long ago retreated from yellows and oranges and shades of striking blue and purple to browns and blacks and dirty whites. Petals and pieces of petals and flowers fell to the table as nervous hands arranged and rearranged the bouquet. Next, she turned to her mother's geranium, struggling to stay alive under the rationed water Jo Anne was able to give it, taken from her own meager rations, hiding the plant from inspectors when they came. Luis was unaware of the tear that escaped from the corner of his wife's eye until she wiped it away with her forefinger and smeared it on a geranium leaf, not wanting to waste the liquid.

"Jo Anne!" Luis yelled, angry again. "I work all day and come home to…well, nothing! Why is supper not ready? Why do you not answer me?" He sat the champagne carefully on the window sill, not wanting it to fall and break. "I am your husband! You keep going on like this, and you never answer me. Now tell me, what is the matter? I cannot help if you will not talk to me."

Jo Anne continued fussing with the geranium and the dried flowers, a faraway look in her eyes, then, disgusted, she swept her hands over the fallen pieces of dried flowers, sending them fluttering to the cold sandstone floor.

"Jose Rodriquez died in the

infirmary this morning," she said, hunching over, leaning on the table with both hands, her voice low and unsteady. "From his wounds from the accident. That's three from the mines in the last two weeks, Luis. Three!"

"I know. I work there, remember? Part of the roof caved in. Rodriquez was in the wrong place. The same thing happened to Douglas and Michael. Miriam died of cancer. It happens. You knew those kinds of things could happen before we came here. We all did. It is part of the price!"

Jo Anne's hands began to shake. She turned from the flowers and faced Luis, determined to say what she had to say.

"I...I want to go home," she blurted, tears forming in her eyes, her hands flying to her face, trying to hide the anguish there, the feeling of guilt, trying to hide the tears.

"*What?*" Luis was dumbfounded.

"The *Propitious* entered Mars orbit two days ago. You know that. They will be going back to Earth in a week or so, once they are reloaded," Jo Anne said. She pulled a handkerchief from her coat pocket and blew her nose, then wiped at more tears with the back of her hand. She looked steadfastly at her husband of five years. "She only comes once every year or so, in rotation with the *Earthstar*. I...I'm going home with those that have finished out their contract here."

"You crazy *gringa*!" Luis exploded. "What the hell are you talking about? Men die. Women die. So what? I feel bad, you feel bad, we all feel bad. You think the corporation is going to pay us this kind of money if there is no danger? These things happen! Those three men, their people back home, they will be well compensated. The bodies will be put in a deep freeze and transported back. Miriam was buried here on Mars—as was her wish, having no family back on Earth—out there in our little cemetery, out there with the others."

Taking deep breaths, Luis calmed himself. He walked to the window, then turned and looked back at his wife, into her tear-filled eyes. "You are worried about me, right?" he asked in soft tones, bewildered.

"No, that's not it!" Jo Anne said, knotting her hands into tiny fists again, clenching and unclenching them at her stomach. "Maybe…maybe just a little bit."

"Then what? You know we cannot leave for over a year yet if we are to get our money. Why are you saying this?"

"We can leave anytime the ships come. They always have room! They leave far more than they ever take back. You know that." Jo Anne searched her husband's eyes, her hands quiet, knowing she'd hurt him, shaken him bad. She fought back more tears, her eyes pleading.

Luis moved from the window and walked the few short feet to where Jo Anne stood by the table. He stared at the wall behind her, the sandstone brick wall with the room's one small picture of a home and its surroundings hanging on it, the only one they'd been allowed to have — corporation issue, the only picture in the whole damn place. It showed green billowing grasses and green, majestic pine and other trees on a bluff backed by a deep blue ocean. An old, well-kept, wooden house, painted white, stood on a hill away from the bluff, surrounded by a white picket fence and colorful flowers, a garden out back, vines on the walls. His dream, his wife's dream. He stared at her for a brief moment, then turned and looked out the window.

"Sure. Sure we can leave," he said, his back to Jo Anne. "And I can go back to picking oranges and lemons in the heat and lettuce in the cold and the fog, and maybe you can get a job again as a maid or dish-wipe in some sleaze joint back there in Fresno, and we can suck up to the people who own the ranches and hotels and try to hide our shame again, to swallow our pride. And, if we are really, really lucky, maybe, just maybe, we can make enough to keep from starving ourselves and living in a trailer again.

You are forgetting something here. Did you forget that we forfeit all of our money if we leave even one day before our two years here are up? The money that is supposed to set us free so we do not have to live like street dogs for the rest of our lives. Did you forget that?"

"No, I didn't forget!" Jo Anne answered, her face twisted, looking at her lover, her best friend, the strong, handsome man that had worked so hard for her over the years. "But…but even if I stayed to get the money, Luis, it wouldn't change the way I feel. I…I feel like I'm dying here."

"Oh?" Luis said, at a loss for words. He turned to face his wife, a hollow in his stomach that was beginning to ache. "Is this why you have been so down the last few months? Because you want to go back? Is this why we do not make love no more, why you stay clear of me?"

"Oh, Luis," Jo Anne said, searching his eyes, her heart breaking. "I know what being here means to you. I don't want to hurt you."

"You already done that!" Luis exploded again. "Where are you going to live if you go back? You got no money and no family."

"My aunt—"

"She kicked you out the last time! Remember? Because you were going out with me! Shame on you, dating a Mex! That is one reason we got married, remember? Because we loved each other, we needed each other. We had nobody but us. Cannot you understand why we came here? We came to Mars so someday we could go to school and be somebody. Why can you not understand this?

Now you want to throw away the only chance we got because you do not love me anymore? You do not have to love me if you do not want to, Jo. That is okay. I was used to that before we met. I will sleep down here. You can sleep up there. But let us not throw away all we got going for us. We do not get any second chance here. You know? You got no place to go back on Earth anyway! Wake up!"

Jo Anne averted her eyes, looking past her husband to the opposite wall. "I never said I don't love you, Luis. I love you more than anything. It's just that…. It's just that I can't take this… this place anymore. I'm no good here. Can't you see? I don't belong."

"What? What about this place? It is not so bad here, even with the cold. They pay for everything; the food, the rent, our clothes, everything but beer and pretzels. I have been in worse places back on Earth, and so have you. What is it you cannot take? I do not understand. We can work this out, Jo. I know we can."

Jo Anne pointed toward the window with her right hand, her left still knotted at her waist. "I can't take this godforsaken desert world anymore, Luis! There's nothing to look at except rocks and sand and that godawful dead volcano. All the same ugly colors every day and every night. Nothing ever changes! We can't go outside, and there's nothing inside anymore, and even if we could go outside, there's no place to go. Everybody works so damn hard to stay here, to not get fired or hurt and sent back. Six days a week, every week, even if you're half-dead from the flu. People die in the mines or get crippled. What kind of life is that? It's okay for the terraformers and NASA to be here. That's what they want to do. To them, Mars is one great, grand adventure. It's their life and their world. But it's not mine. Nothing here is mine! Not this house, not the furniture, the blankets, nothing! Just my mother's half-dead geranium."

"You knew what you were in for when you signed up!" Luis shouted, angry again. "Everybody did! And besides, *I am* yours! Do not I count anymore?"

"What happened to our park, Luis?" Jo Anne shouted back, ignoring his question. "Our park with running water, and a little lake, and trees and flowers, and our victory garden? They promised me! It was written in the contract! It's the main reason I thought I could survive here. I'm a

human being, for Christ's sake, Luis!
A child of Earth, not of Mars!"

"It is not my fault that the space
mirror got shredded, Jo, or that the
engineers did not make it better the
first time! Or construct enough of
them! For the love of God, Jo, wait
awhile. Sparaxis sent the spare parts
and materials we need to repair the
space mirror on the *Propitious*. They
have been unloading them onto the
Odyssey and bringing them down,
and UNTO has sent an extra man
and a woman, both experts, to help
repair the mirror and get the job done
more quickly. They need the water
for here and to build more places
as Mars grows. More greenhouses,
expand the mines, another domed
city in the planning. They have the
money. When the materials get
unloaded, they will fix everything,

just like new, and we will have the water we need again. And we will have the spare parts for the nuclear power plants and materials to build another mirror to shine on and help keep Bradbury Base warm. Materials for some new greenhouses — those are on the *Propitious* too. You know that. It will not be so cold here within the next few months or so. You have to be patient. New plants and seeds too, to replant the park and…and the victory gardens."

"You don't understand!" Jo Anne said, turning toward Luis, the tears coming again. "I need some *Earth*! Now! Not six months down the road, or a year, or whatever. What good are the seeds and plants if we have no water for them? Who knows how long it will take to fix the mirror, to install the new one? What if it gets shredded again? I need plants, green things, flowers, birds, something to tell me why I came here and what's waiting for me when I get home. I'm not like you. I can't keep watching the same old videos, or go to the bar, or play ball in that sandy waste of a park, or go to the gym. There aren't that many women here, and when the girls and I go out together—when we go anywhere—the men stare at us. Even where we work. It…it's embarrassing and debasing."

"What is wrong with that? You are all worth staring at," Luis said.

"Stop it! Would you please try and understand me for once in your life? I need more! I need a rainbow, waves pounding on a beach, a bird, bright colored trees in the fall, rain. I've tried so hard, Luis. When they shut down the plumbing, that was okay. I could manage, running to the outhouses, freezing my butt off. But when they wouldn't let me water my garden and told me not to water my geranium anymore, it took the heart out of me. It is all I had from my mother, my family. I have to hide it whenever the inspectors come! Even then, I kept trying, but something won't let me live here, something vital. I'm sorry, Luis, but something is missing, and I'm not cut out for this. If I miss this ship going home, I'll dry up and die here, just like everything else. I have to go." Jo Anne looked into Luis's eyes, wanting him to understand. "Come with me," she pleaded. "We'll be okay." She wiped more tears from her eyes. "Please. I'll work hard back home, get two or three jobs, whatever it takes. I promise."

"You are going to do it then?"

Luis asked, stunned, barely able to speak. "You are going to throw away four hundred thousand dollars and any real chance we had when we got back to Earth? You are going to be perfectly happy to see me sweat in the fields for the rest of my life and die before my time? And you? You are going back to cleaning toilets and sweeping floors for a living? Do you like that? Jo, you are acting crazy and selfish. All you care about is you."

"That's not fair! There are more things to life than money, Luis! Please try and understand."

"Oh, I understand okay. You are running out on me and our future and our children. Well, you go on ahead, *gringa*. I do not care no more." Numb and hurt, Luis started for the door, wiping at his own tears now.

"Luis, *please*," Jo Anne continued

to plead, her hands tied in knots again. "I don't want to go back alone, not without you." She watched as her husband jerked his overcoat from the closet and stormed out the door, slamming it behind him.

"Luis! Where are you going?" she screamed at the door, then jerked around and stared out the window again, full of hate for the red, rocky, ugly planet. It had taken her soul, and now it was taking her husband. She spit at the glass, smeared the spit, hard, as far as it would smear, spit again, trying to blot out the view, then climbed the ladder up to her bedroom, crying her heart out.

CHAPTER 6

Jimmy's Saloon

"What am I going to do?" Luis asked. He gazed around the small, dowdy, dimly lit bar to the small, empty dance floor beyond the silver and gold dangling beads. Luis sought company, someone he knew, but only he and the bartender shared the two rooms. Neon lights fizzed and popped overhead and behind the bar, most of them turned off or down due to the energy crisis. Jimmy Serrano, all five-foot-eight and 246 pounds of him, mostly fat, shrugged and wiped at a glass tucked under what was left of his right arm. He wore a bright yellow and blue apron around his stomach and a worn cowboy hat on his head, the one item he was allowed to bring along to Mars with him as a luxury.

Luis cradled a bottle of beer on the counter, looking to Jimmy for answers. On a far wall was a print of Earth, the same print that was on Luis's wall in his row house, the same print that hung in almost every corporation apartment and every corporation building on Bradbury Base. A scratchy string played "Home on the Range."

"We had it all planned, Jimmy," Luis said. "Go to Mars for two years, three, more or less, counting out and back. Get our four-hundred-grand they pay us here and maybe the bonus too.

Maybe even five-hundred-thousand with the bonus, man, between me and Jo! Half a million bucks, man! Go home, go to college, make something of ourselves, you know? A kid from the wrong side of the tracks and a kid no one wanted, making it big for all to see. Now my crazy wife wants to go home. Can you believe that? We will lose everything! I will go back to picking grapes in the hot sun, and she will go back to cleaning rooms and toilets. What kind of a life is that, Jimmy? We were lucky to come here with all the people applying. Where is a guy with hardly no school going to make this kind of money on Earth, especially a cowboy like me, huh?"

Jimmy, used to listening to tales of woe, shrugged in sympathy and continued to clean glasses.

"You got to help me here!"

Luis said, becoming angry. He stood up and reached over the counter, grabbing Jimmy by the front of his shirt and staring into his eyes. "Come on, man, you have got to tell me what to do."

Jimmy, almost twice the size of Luis, pried the hand from his shirt. "Come on, Luis, calm down. Getting mad at me won't solve your problem."

Frowning, Luis pulled his hand back, looked at it, then to Jimmy and spoke, bewildered. "I am sorry, Jimmy. *Dios mio.* I am going *loco.*"

"Do you love her?" Jimmy asked after Luis had sat back down after he'd finished his beer and ordered another.

"Of course I love her. What kind of a question is that? You think I would bring her all the way to this red rock if I didn't? If *she* didn't love me?"

Jimmy set a glass down and

fumbled with the apron around his ample middle. "I'm only trying to help, *amigo*. You asked, remember?"

"Yeah. I am sorry, man. It was just a stupid question."

Jimmy grunted and scratched at his beard with his left hand. He'd lost the other in a mining accident eleven months ago, but when he'd been offered the bartending job after the previous bartender was on his way back to Earth, he had decided to stick out his tour of duty. Two hundred thousand dollars was a powerful incentive, even if some of the men and women never lived to see it. That, on top of his insurance money, should set him up for life back home. *If* he decided to go.

"A lot of people go back early, Luis," Jimmy counseled, "for a lot of reasons. It sounds like your wife has the most common one: she's downright homesick. It's a common human element, especially with women. You've got to let her go, or she'll just get worse. She could wither away, maybe commit suicide. We've had a few of those, you know, over the years. The latest was that Harper woman a while back. Not just the women, either. I see a lot of guys down, way down, trying to drink their troubles away. It's been that way since the lake dried up and all the plants died. The people from NASA and UNTO, they don't come here much anymore. Afraid of more fighting, I guess, over the water issues, and other things. This bar has become one little deserted, gloomy place. If any of our other reactors go down before the others get fixed…. Well, we got a real big problem, especially at night. Way, way big. You'da thought the corporation would've anticipated such problems and stored more supplies than they did for just such emergencies."

"Come on, Jimmy! Now you are sounding like my Jo Anne!"

"You brought the subject up, my friend."

"Well, change it, would you?"

Jimmy frowned, sat the glass behind the counter, and picked up another one. "I heard they found more red diamonds in the south mine yesterday. Huge. Half as big as my fist. And another gold vein in the north mine."

"Yeah? I already knew that. So what?"

"There are very few red diamonds on Earth, Luis. Did you forget? And gold is almost impossible to find there anymore. Do you ever

think of where the money comes
from to keep us here, to keep the
mines running, to pay us when we go
home — *if* we go home?"

"It comes from the rare
diamonds, and the more common
ones too, and the gold, and other
rocks found here, Jimmy! You think I
am stupid? What are you getting at?"

"Well, these aren't ordinary
diamonds. It may be hard to believe,
but Mars diamonds are harder than
any found on Earth. Something to
do with the size of Olympus Mons,
its weight. Their industrial strength
alone is enough to make mining here
profitable. But the colors! Reds and
greens and blues and oranges! Pure,
mixed colors. There are people on
Earth willing to pay millions for those
colors, Luis, people with big money.
You know that? A handful of Mars

diamonds is almost enough to pay everyone working for Sparaxis a year's wage. Not to mention the platinum and other rare Mars stuff. Sparaxis is making a mint here."

"Who would have thought of diamonds on Mars, eh?" Luis asked, glad the subject was changing.

"Why not? They're formed under tremendous pressure, crystallized out of carbon, and Mars had plenty of all three way back when the volcanoes were active. There's probably diamonds and other precious metals all over the place here. That's why Sparaxis wants to get this planet going, not shut Mars down like the diamond people back on Earth want their governments to do. Old man Sparaxis has all but closed those guys down. South Africa is in a big financial mess last I heard. The old man likes a fight, all right. And here, on Mars? Shoot, Sparaxis is the only game in town, and things will stay that way if the old man has anything to do with it. When he gets things going better here, it's off to the other planets and moons. Lotsa room out there for more people."

"Tell me then, Jimmy — if they are making so damn much money, how come we cannot get any water?"

"Because UNTO has been running all the terraforming crap or trying to. They are the ones most in charge of those operations, and to be fair, the most qualified and dedicated. And, if you will remember, Sparaxis is helping to fund their operation, so UNTO really can't do anything to shut the mines down, even though they'd like to. Now that the corporation has pitched in and will be helping with the terraforming and helping to restore the space mirror, along with building another one with all those supplies that came in on the *Propitious*, things on Mars are going to jump. Everyone working together, they'll get it done in half the time. I hear one reason Sparaxis is helping with the terraforming is because things are going too slow for him. Old man Max is going to own the whole damn planet someday. Imagine that. Maybe the whole damn solar system if he lives long enough. You wait and see. The water and other stuff will just take time. They're talking about mining the ice asteroids again. We'll see how that goes. We've got to do a better job of getting this planet going, Luis, somewhere for some of those billions of people back home to move to. Otherwise, Mother Earth is not going to make it. Like I said, Mars will be a launching pad to other planets someday. You just wait and see."

"But I do not have any time, Jimmy. I have been trying to tell you that!"

Jimmy turned a deaf ear. A wistful look filled his eyes. "I've been thinking about staying on, you know? Staying over when my two years are up. Be a Martian." Jimmy laughed.

"You are joking, right?" Luis said, not believing. He finished his beer and ordered another. "Why?" he asked when he saw that Jimmy was serious.

"Why not?" Jimmy shrugged. "I've got nobody back home, like most everyone else here. Like you and Jo Anne! I've got a good job, and it doesn't wear me out like the mines did, and who wants a guy with only one good arm anyway? Mars is going to grow, Luis. If the planet goes into more private hands, and it looks like it's headed that way, things will go faster. In fifty or a hundred years or so, Mars may have enough atmospheric pressure so people can walk on the surface with only breathing masks and radiation suits, not those bulky things we have to wear now. When it's warm enough, anyway, and the new space mirror should help with that, especially around the base here, and maybe more mirrors someday, and more space ships!

"There will be plants and a breathable atmosphere in two-hundred years maybe, as least as good as in the Andes back on Earth. We'll have rain and free-flowing water. Can you imagine what a waterfall would look like on Mars, Luis, with her lighter gravity? The wind whipping spray all over the place! Think of the football games. Tennis. Baseball! You could throw a ball a mile here. Hit one a mile too! How tall do you think the trees will grow in light gravity, Luis? A redwood? A thousand feet? Two thousand? It's exciting now, and it can only get better."

"Yeah, then how come I'm not excited?"

"Because you're a sourpuss!"

Luis squinched his eyes, scratched his head, frowned, and said nothing.

"There's enough water here, all right, locked up in the polar caps and underground ice," Jimmy continued. "We'll find other aquifers, too, maybe lots of them, and big ones. With both poles melting, they keep putting a lot of CO_2 and H_2O in the air. Lots of people at NASA and UNTO don't like us very much, Luis. Maybe they ripped the mirror on purpose, hoping we'd move! They don't want us mining here, say we're ruining the planet. Give me a break! But it's already a little warmer here because of it, and some of the CO2 in the ground is coming out and putting more air in the atmosphere. Just before you and Jo Anne came here, we got clouds high up on the mountain. Real clouds, not those funky Martian wave things, or convectives, or…. Sorry, I forgot what you call them."

"You know a lot about things here," Luis said, impressed.

"Yeah, thanks. I've been here a while, Luis, and I hear a lot running this place. Like I was saying, they were *real* clouds, like back on Earth. Called them cumulus nymphos or something like that. Funny name for a cloud, huh? Anyway, there was lightning and everything. Some say it was the first Earth-type storm Mars has had, at least the first one in a million years or more, or whatever. We can't really know because we haven't been here that long, haven't figured out the science. Anyway, those clouds left a huge ring of snow up on old Olympus Mons, maybe six or seven miles up. The mountain up there looked like a big, white donut. It sure was pretty and lasted a long time. The scientists said it was water ice, just like back home, and it had something to do with the terraforming now that the north and south polar caps are melting, or at least the south cap now."

"Yeah, I remember people saying that," Luis said, a faraway look in his eyes. Visions of snowfields back home danced through his head, but only for a moment. Luis's hands squeezed his glass, and his knuckles turned white. He held onto his glass for dear life as if he was falling, and it was the only thing he had to hold on to. Tears rolled down his bronzed cheeks. Luis lowered his head, ashamed to be crying. He let go of the glass, pushed it away, leaned his elbows on the counter, and covered his face with his hands, already missing Jo Anne.

"I cannot go back, Jimmy," Luis said, shaking his head. He wiped at his eyes. "There is nothing for me there. I would die on Earth now, same as Jo Anne would die here. If only I did not love her so much! What am I supposed to do?"

Jimmy's lips tightened. He bent over and patted Luis's heaving shoulders, then felt relief as a small group of miners, five men and a woman, banged through the door and made their way to the bar, shouting and laughing and having a good time.

CHAPTER 7

Mars Calling

Jo Anne came down early the next morning to find Luis still asleep on the plastic sofa. Jimmy and three other men had brought him home last night, drunk out of his head, and put him there on her instructions. He'd passed out almost immediately, never saying a word to her, never even glancing her way. She didn't try to wake him, only covered him with a wool blanket to keep him warm. She'd talk to him later and make a last attempt at persuading him to go home with her.

Next, she called the shuttle port office. Yes, they had a vacant cubicle for the return trip. There were several — due to the deaths the past year, the bodies would be placed in the cold storage lockers. She would have to come over and fill out the necessary forms and sign the forfeiture papers.

It was dark and cold under the dome when she exited the apartment, adding to her misery. Another dust storm, she thought, the only weather the ugly planet had to offer. Jo Anne kept her eyes glued to the walkway as she crossed through the park to the office, not wanting to view her bleak surroundings. Visions of green fields, blue oceans, and snow-capped peaks pirouetted in her mind. Flowers and trees, blue skies, rain and white picket fences, eagles and doves and bluebirds, dogs and cats, children, and Luis. No smile crossed her face.

She returned several hours later to find Luis gone. Probably gone to work, she thought.

Her heart sickness worsened. She'd hoped and prayed that he'd stay home, that they could talk, work something out. What if he didn't come home tonight, choosing instead to stay at the infirmary or at the mines? She might have to leave without ever seeing him again, without ever saying goodbye. Jo Anne climbed the upladder and, with trembling hands and new tears, packed the few small belongings she'd brought with her. One small suitcase in, one small suitcase out—the company had provided everything else. Aside from a bag full of bad memories and her few personnel possessions and precious geranium, packed and ready to go, she wouldn't be taking much of anything else home, especially any damn Martian souvenirs.

When she was finished, and her tears had subsided, and for want of anything else to do, Jo Anne sat down and turned on the room's little computer, hoping for some news from Earth. Instead, she got the Mars weather station, located at UNTO's station on the south side of the mountain, its seventy-five-foot antenna array anchored on a rock outcropping high up. Jo Anne glanced out the window, noticing it had grown darker. She thought of going outside to look, but the station's broadcaster, a young, pretty black woman Jo Anne recognized as Kimberly James, one of UNTO's meteorologists, began to shout.

"Good Morning Mars!" she said, smiling, her voice radiating enthusiasm and vitality. By her looks, Jo Anne figured the announcer was around twenty-seven or twenty-eight. "Sorry to interrupt your regular programming, but this morning we have had some unusual weather we thought you folks out there would like to hear about. Actually, what you need to know! Now that the sun is coming up, clouds, real clouds, have formed over the South Pole and are moving in our direction! When this cold front hits the warming surface of our surrounding territory, we could have a moisture drop. That's right, folks. I'm talking about possible rain and snow! Maybe even down here on the damn ground! Stay tuned because this front is headed our way right now. Fast! Say your prayers. Yahoo!"

Jo Anne didn't wait to hear the rest. Forgetting her problems for a moment, she hurried to the window, then cleaned it and peered out, watching as a scattering of puffy clouds raced by overhead. The darkness hadn't been just another dust storm after all, but a combination of weather factors. Looking south, she saw the heavy line of storm clouds moving her way, the most beautiful mix of white, gray, and pink she'd ever seen. Lightning flared along the storm wall. Smatterings of dust and sand swirled ahead of the front, blowing down the valley and beginning to obscure the mining complex at the base of Olympus Mons. Jo Anne could hardly breathe. Her pulse quickened.

"Luis? Where are you? It's going to rain!" she yelled at the empty rooms.

"Oh, you wouldn't care anyway, Mister Mars Man," she muttered to herself after several seconds had passed, realizing he wasn't there. She fought down her anguish, went to the closet and put on a heavy coat with a hood, then left the apartment. The dome felt warmer than usual, almost comfortable with the rising sun lighting it up. Jo Anne took off her coat, tucked it under her arm, and ran past her block of row houses until she came to a wide opening separating her block from the one north of her. She ran between the buildings, stumbling across dead garden plants and sidestepping tomato cages and plant stakes to reach the dome wall. There were already dozens of people milling about, some from the early morning shift of workers, some of the 270 or so people that would be going home tomorrow or the next day, their contracts with Sparaxis complete, and some of the 270 souls that had just arrived, wondering what the hell was going on and why everyone was so excited. Jo Anne's side of the dome was packed—everyone seemed happy. A few pressed their hands and noses against the curve of the dome, trying to get a better view. There was a lot of shoving and jostling, but no one seemed to mind.

They all gazed toward the pinkish-gray wall down the valley, pushing its way toward them. People stared, eyes wide, spellbound and holding their breaths. A deathly silence fell over the dome. No one spoke.

Within the next several minutes, more people walked, ran, or stumbled from their homes and offices to

see what was going on, and soon
there was a huge crowd of people
milling about near the dome walls.
Nervous voices began to babble.
There was an electricity in the air, a
human electricity, generated by an
anticipation of something that hadn't
happened for who knew how long.
Jo Anne craned her neck and stood
on her toes, hoping to spot Luis in
the crowd, but to no avail. She stood
flat-footed again, trying not to let her
husband's absence spoil the moment.

More quiet and restless minutes
passed. The massive storm continued
to rush north, engulfing the nearby
hills and valleys while approaching
the bulk of Olympus Mons. Soon the
mining complex disappeared beneath
the raging sand and dust running
ahead of the clouds. The dome grew
dark and eerie as the billowing clouds

began to suffocate the sun rising to the south.

They waited. A man shouted, "It's going to be dry fun, folks! Like the desert storms on Earth, all clouds and no rain. It's too dry here!"

Boos and jeers echoed from the gathering.

"Pessimist!" a man shouted.

"Get lost, loser!" a woman shrieked.

Disappointment shrouded the crowd. The clouds continued their northward journey and soon were obscuring most of the mountain. Happy, excited faces began turning sour when a trio of lightning bolts pierced the Martian sky, startling everyone. Eyes were being rubbed, and heads were shaking when the crash of thunder sounded throughout the city, jiggling its walls like Jell-O, scaring some and thrilling others.

"Look!" a woman shouted, someone close to Jo Anne, so loud it sent her eardrums humming. "It's rain! Oh my dear God, it is, it is!"

Everyone's head turned in unison from where the woman stood and pointed. Eyes peered upward. Specks of darkness appeared in the fine layer of dust on the outside dome wall, sending up small, mushroom shaped puffs of dust. Soon more and bigger drops fell, then a deluge of rain. The dome walls ran pinkish-red for brief moments, in streaks and curving lines and little rivers. Then the wall flushed clean, showing a clarity that hadn't been seen since the dome was first completed. All across the valley, rain fell in huge, wind-driven sheets. Dust settled, mud formed, people cheered and screamed. They jumped and danced. It was all of Earth's holidays rolled into one. Men and women ran to their apartments in long strides, airborne gazelles in the one-third Earth gravity. They quickly returned with precious hoarded wines and fancy canned foods. Soon others made similar trips, bringing special items with them, saved for just such an occasion on occasionless Mars.

"Oh my," Jo Anne whispered when a tall man whisked her off her feet, giving her hugs and kisses and twirling her around. He put Jo Anne back down, handed her a plastic cup, and poured her some wine. She thanked him and, blushing, drank the whole thing in one gulp.

People shared what little they had, their wines and whiskeys, dehydrated sausages and ham. Music suddenly blared out over the corporation's loudspeakers: loud, wild, New-Front, Rip-Rap, and old classics. Strangers danced with strangers. Gender didn't matter — whoever was close enough to snag got snagged. Noses pressed against the bubble wall in disbelief. The dome pulsed and rattled, dancing to the thunder and music along with its inhabitants. Rivulets formed in the ageless Martian soil, only to be devoured by the arid planet. Super oxides in the valley soil dissolved and lost their toxicity. More lightning crossed the sky, setting the hills and the mountain's cliffs on fire. Thunder boomed, and people did crazy things as the rain continued to fall. Sweet, beautiful, lukewarm heavy rainfall rinsed and decontaminated the ancient sands and rocks and hills.

The storm ended all too quickly.

The din on the roof quieted, then was gone. The main body of clouds scurried past, hell-bent for some unknown destination, dissipating as they went. Puffs of straggler clouds hurried after, trying to catch up. Then the sun flooded the valley, the mountain and Bradbury Base and all around it, sunlight so bright people had to shield their eyes. Snow ringed Olympus Mons from six to ten miles up and covered the top of the escarpment, along with the higher of the nearby hills and plateaus. The city's ring of humanity stood spellbound yet again, gazing out upon a different world, their revelry forgotten. The music faded and stopped as the last raindrop skidded to the ground. A sad, profound quiet settled over the dome.

"Man, that was quick," a man

standing close to Jo Anne said softly, then shouted, "It's over, folks! But what a show, eh? Hey, everybody! What a wonderful, beautiful show! We are a part of history now!"

Some laughed at this, some clapped, some jumped up and down, others began to cry. The folks that had been stationed there a long time felt a stirring in their souls that they hadn't experienced since leaving Earth. The crowd milled around for a while. The last drinks were poured, the last candy eaten. People tried to hide their sadness and spoke in whispers as the last clouds, headed north, disappeared, sucked dry by the endless Martian deserts. Soon the crowd retreated to their row houses or offices, putting on their coats as the forgotten cold again began penetrating the dome and their hearts.

Jo Anne, her spirits sagging, was one of the last to leave. She stared out at the emptiness for a long time, strange feelings within her she couldn't fathom, worse than before. She felt a whirlwind of mixed emotions, torn between going home and leaving the man she loved or staying and slugging it out. It had rained. The mountain and hills were breathtaking with their blanket of white, and maybe, just maybe, someday, some year, some century, it might rain and snow again. And then again, it might not. But, as for now, at long last, it appeared that the terraforming was working. Jo Anne smiled for the first time since she couldn't remember when.

She tore herself from the wall and its now spectacular scenery, the desert now colored a deep, brick red, realizing that the desolate world had somehow managed to steal a place in her heart, never to leave, welcoming her, asking her to stay, not to give up on Mars, even though she thought she'd shut the door to this planet long ago. Still, even with the clouds and the rain and their almost spiritual quality, she realized she couldn't stay. Soon the hills and the mountain would be dry, the dust and sand would blow again, and she'd become as homesick and depressed as ever.

She walked home, slowly and alone, her head down and her shoulders hunched. Once there, she found Luis passed out on the sofa, a small, empty bottle of cheap wine clutched in his right hand, cradled on his chest. He had missed it all.

"Oh, Luis," she admonished herself. "It's me who made you miss it. It's me who is always messing up your life." She tiptoed over and patted him on the shoulder, kissed his forehead, careful not to wake him, then turned and climbed the upladder. She'd take a nap, say goodbye to Luis when he awakened, and then spend her last night on Mars at the infirmary. There her friends and coworkers, those not going home, promised to give her, and the others leaving, a farewell party.

Jo Anne lay down and was quickly asleep, exhausted from the morning's excitement and her deepening torment. She dreamed of clouds and rain, bluebirds and bees. And Luis. A young, proud, strong, and loving Luis, laughing and holding their babies in his arms, a white house with blue trim and a white picket fence and flowers and trees in the background, birds and butterflies and dogs and cats and all those things. Jo

Anne smiled in her sleep.

* * *

Jo Anne awakened with a start as if someone had slapped her face.

"Luis!" she cried out. Something had happened to her husband. She jumped from the bed and hurried to the downladder, only to find him gone. Jo Anne read the note telling her he'd called in sick to the mines and gone into town, saying he didn't want to see her anymore and didn't want to say farewell. She crumpled the note and threw it on the floor, grinding it into the sandstone. Despondent, she opened a can of soup, only to find she wasn't hungry. She sighed, stored the soup, and walked back to the main room. Jo Anne stood, her arms crossed, next to the window and the bottle of champagne, still corked and perched precariously on the sill. She looked out, the thought of the long, grueling, dangerous, monotonous trip home crowding her mind, and then her mouth fell open.

"Oh my God!" she screamed, blinking to make sure she was awake. Jo Anne pinched herself, but the image didn't disappear. It wasn't a dream or an illusion. As far as she could see, from the edge of the dome to the far off snow lines, from north of the valley to the southern plains, there was a solid mat of bright-green *something*, contrasting sharply with the mountain, the white hills, and the pink Martian sky.

"It's not possible," Jo Anne gasped, her breath all but gone. She surmised that the undulating green sea was some kind of plant life, not knowing how it got there and not caring. She only knew that the transfixing beauty was filling a void in her heart that had existed since she'd arrived on Mars. There *was* life here.

She wondered why the Martian plants had never made an appearance in Bradbury Base or in the greenhouses where, at least in the past, there had been ample water to water the park grounds and enough overflow to wet the greenhouse floors. After a few minutes, Jo Anne surmised the base, and all it entailed, had been graded off before any building had taken place, no doubt shoving any Martian seeds and spores off into the canyons and culverts that surrounded the dome.

Staring at the impossible panorama before her, Jo Anne realized she'd been acting like a baby ever since they'd landed. She just hadn't had the wisdom, or the patience, to see the beauty that existed on the Red

Planet and its possibilities.

She felt shame for wallowing in her self-pity for so long, letting it destroy the things she cherished and loved most: her love of life, her love for others, and most of all, her love for Luis. What did it matter where you lived as long as you were loved and loved in return?

Jo Anne reveled in the rolling green valley, the snow-clad hills and the mountain, sparkling now beneath the slanting rays of distant Sol. She gazed past Olympus Mons to the distant, curving skyline, and for the second time that day, felt the Red Planet's mysterious pull. To Jo Anne, Mars seemed somehow happy, as if rejoicing in some distant remembrance, as if giving her a glimpse of things to come. She realized the rain and snow might never again fall in her lifetime, the clouds might never race across the skies, but there was hope for humanity, hope for Mars, and most of all, hope for her and Luis, and that was enough.

* * *

Jo Anne was jarred from her reverie when the front door slammed. Turning, she watched as Luis stalked into the room and stared at her, his bloodshot eyes betraying defeat.

"Luis, I—"

"Not now, Jo, please. I have got things to do upladder. Just leave me alone."

"But—?"

Jo Anne walked over and slumped into one of the plastic chairs, despondent again as Luis climbed the ladder and disappeared. She gazed out the window. Her vision blurred with tears, tears she had vowed not to shed again.

Jo Anne didn't know how long it was before Luis came back down. He stood at the bottom of the ladder, holding on to one rung with his left hand while carrying his little suitcase in his right. His shoulders were stooped, and there was a look of resignation in his eyes.

"Luis, please, *please* don't leave. I...I—"

"I am not leaving you, Jo," he said, his voice cracking. "I am going back to Earth with you. God help me, but I cannot live without you. You are worth much more to me than any amount of money."

Jo Anne rose from her chair, ran to Luis, jumped into his arms, hugged him, and then began kissing him all over his face, neck, and head. "No need, my big, strong, handsome man," she whispered in his ear between kisses. "I'm staying."

* * *

That evening the Martian plants, similar to Earth mosses and lichens, likenesses of Earth's arctic hair grass and pearlwort, curled in on themselves to survive the oncoming freezing night. When the first rays of the next day's morning sun topped the horizon, the lichens and mosses uncurled their pseudo fronds and laid them flat against the warming soil, the plants unfolding their leaves to catch the morning sun while producing tiny yellow and purple flowers in the process. There they absorbed the sun's energy and hurried their life processes, knowing that the warmth and moisture wouldn't last long. A gene similar to Earth's SOG1's began repairing plant DNA before it could be destroyed by the sun's damaging ultraviolet light. The gene's goals were to get their hosts through the morning and into their reproductive cycle before the damage became irreparable, killing the plants before they had time to reproduce. Toward midday, millions of tiny, fertile spores on the mosses and lichens, and seeds on the plants, had developed, each with an almost invisible fuzzy, corkscrew tail. A thousand or more spores, or a hundred tiny seeds, would have fit into the palm of a man's hand, each one with a coat as hard as diamonds, having shielded the life within it over the years from the harsh Martian elements.

By late afternoon, with the long rays of Sol sprayed out behind the mountain and far away hills, the mature spores and seeds, moved on

fronds and stalks, rose high into the
air, and were curled and snapped
into the winds, there to be blown and
rolled along, their corkscrew tails
burying them in the softer regions of
the soil, gravity twirling and pulling
them down to a depth of four or five
inches, effectively shielding them from
the sun's harmful rays in the years
to come. There they would patiently
await the next rainfall or outflow, be
it twenty, one hundred, or a million
years from now.

That night the soil moisture
evaporated, sucked dry by the plants
and the aridity that was Mars, the
plants' fronds and leaves and stalks
drying and curling in on themselves
to die. By next morning they had
withered and blown away, tumbled
along the sand, grit, and cobbles,
leaving but a few skeletal shards

lying about, soon to disappear, mute testimony to the tenacity of life.

The valleys and the hills surrounding Bradbury Base turned pink and red once again, the air became choked with grit, and a new layer of fine, pink dust reclaimed the dome.

The Beginning

Gary Carter, a former United States Marine, was born in San Diego, California, where he attended Sweetwater High School, Grossmont College and San Diego State as a science major. He recently retired from a forty-year career as a nursery owner and now lives in the southern Oregon coastal town of Port Orford. He is the author of *Jump Start,* a science fiction thriller concerning the origin of dragons, *For the Good of the Many,* an award-winning national military/political thriller, *The Cedars of Lebanon,* A time travel adventure to ancient Lebanon in an effort to save a war-torn world from further destruction, *Mystic Summer,* a story of young love set in a racially charged southern California town in 1954, the recently released, bestselling *The Beginner's Guide to Growing Herbs and Their Culinary, Medicinal, and Mystical Properties,* and three books of poetry. You can find out more about Gary and his books at his website: garycarterbooksherbs.com

www.ingramcontent.com/pod-product-compliance
Lightning Source LLC
Chambersburg PA
CBHW020133180626
46810CB00004B/1540